To Paul,

Best Wishes!

Good Luck,
Katie Kavanagh

Home Is Where Your Family Is

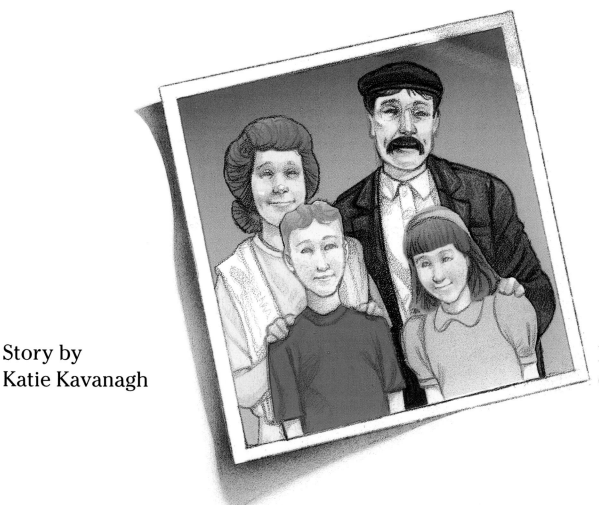

Story by
Katie Kavanagh

Illustrations by
Gregg Fitzhugh

RSVP

RAINTREE
STECK-VAUGHN
PUBLISHERS
The Steck-Vaughn Company

To Mom, Dad, Meghan, and William;
to my friends and all of my teachers,
especially Mrs. Lorraine Field.
Thank you for your love and encouragement. — K.K.

To my children: Austin, Jacob, and Bethany. — G.F.

Printed in Mexico.

1 2 3 4 5 6 7 8 9 0 RRD 98 97 96 95 94 93

Library of Congress Cataloging-in-Publication Data

Kavanagh, Katie, 1982–
    Home is where your family is / written by Katie Kavanagh; illustrated by Gregg Fitzhugh.
        p.   cm. — (Publish-a-book)
    Summary: During the journey from Poland to America, a young girl realizes that although she is leaving one home, she will find another as long as she is with her family.
    ISBN 0–8114–4462–7
    [1. Emigration and immigration — Fiction.   2. Polish Americans — Fiction.
3. Children's writings.]   I. Fitzhugh, Gregg, ill.   II. Title.   III. Series.
PZ7.K1715Ho   1994   93-34497
[Fic] — dc20   CIP
                                                                      AC

I stared back toward land and thought about Poland, the place where I had been born twelve years ago. Though I knew Hitler's army had already burnt down my village outside Gdańsk, I still longed for my tiny house, where the fire was always warm and the food was always delicious. Tears brimmed in my eyes as I thought of the belongings I had to leave behind. We had so little space on the ship that Mama could pack only a few things.

6

"Get off deck before I skin ye alive, ye hear me?" A rough voice interrupted my thoughts.

I ran to the ladder leading down to steerage. I knew quite well I wasn't supposed to be on deck, but steerage was smelly, dark, and crowded. Mama and I shared the top bunk. My older brother, Doniske, and Papa shared the lower, and they took turns watching over our belongings.

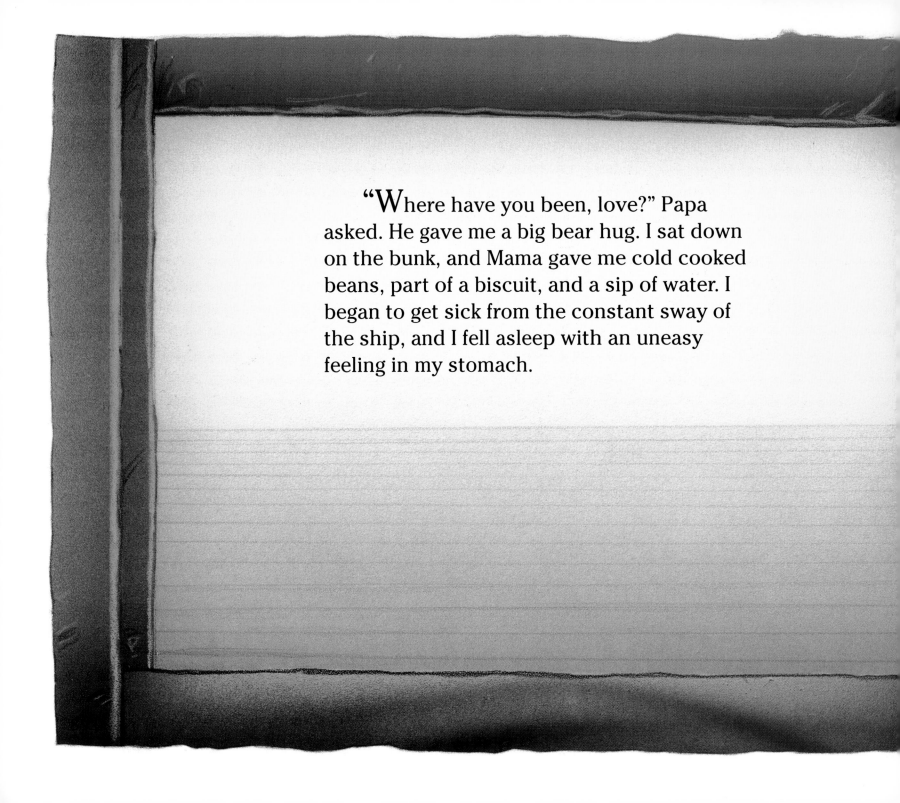

"Where have you been, love?" Papa asked. He gave me a big bear hug. I sat down on the bunk, and Mama gave me cold cooked beans, part of a biscuit, and a sip of water. I began to get sick from the constant sway of the ship, and I fell asleep with an uneasy feeling in my stomach.

9

When I awoke, the uneasy feeling was gone, but it was replaced by a gnawing hunger, even though I hadn't slept long. Mama gave me half of a biscuit, which I decided to eat on deck.

I leaned over the railing at the stern and took a deep breath of the salty air. The wind was strong, the waves high, and I was getting chilly without my shawl.

I didn't want to go back into steerage right away, so I climbed into the center of a coil of rope and settled in. It was comfortable inside, and the wind ruffled the top of my hair.

Soon the world became hazy, and I fell into a deep sleep. In my sleep I was back home, sitting by the fire, Mama knitting by my side. Papa was putting extra logs on the fire, and Doniske was telling us a story.

I woke with a start. Rain was pelting me, and the wind was tearing at every inch of my body, even with the ropes around me. Waves were crashing against the side of the ship, causing a spray of salty water that stung my eyes and tasted awful in my mouth. I heard yelling all around me. "Everyone get below deck!"

I panicked.

I struggled to get out of the rope, but the wet deck was slippery under my boots. Finally I got to my feet and crouched for a moment, not sure of what to do.

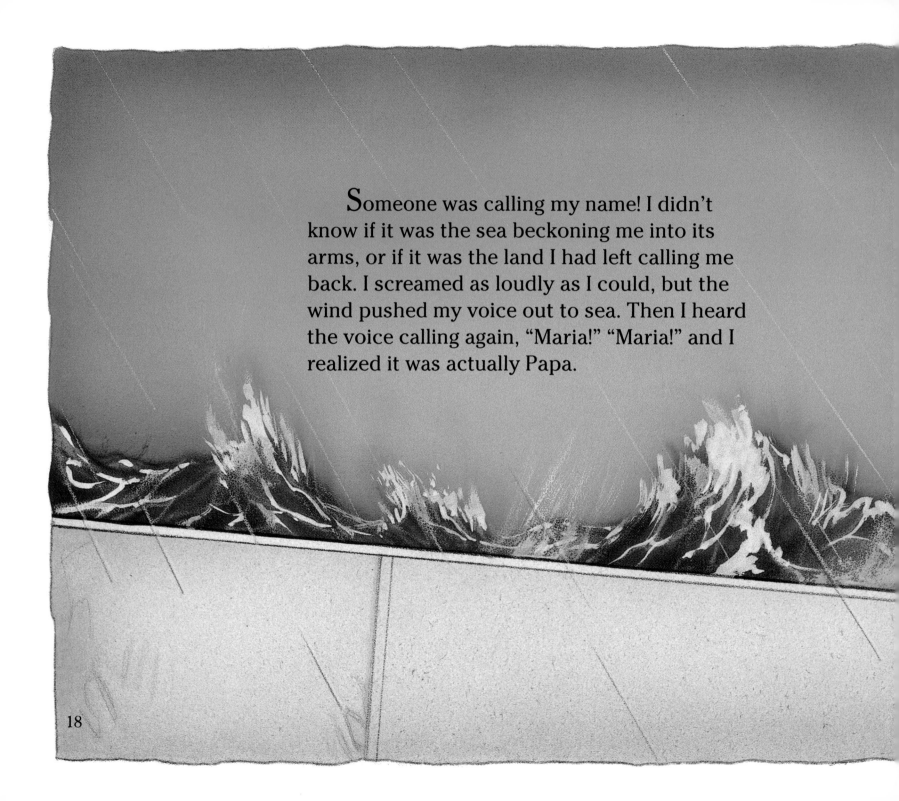

Someone was calling my name! I didn't know if it was the sea beckoning me into its arms, or if it was the land I had left calling me back. I screamed as loudly as I could, but the wind pushed my voice out to sea. Then I heard the voice calling again, "Maria!" "Maria!" and I realized it was actually Papa.

19

20

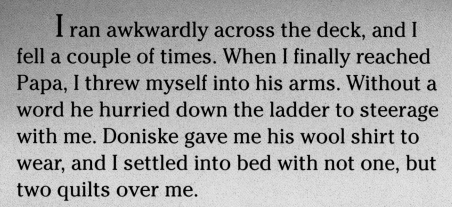

I ran awkwardly across the deck, and I fell a couple of times. When I finally reached Papa, I threw myself into his arms. Without a word he hurried down the ladder to steerage with me. Doniske gave me his wool shirt to wear, and I settled into bed with not one, but two quilts over me.

There was a chain of storms lasting nearly two weeks. Many people got sick, and some even died.

When the sun finally came out, Doniske and I went to sit on deck. As I looked at my brother's pale face, I thought once again of Poland. My eyes filled with tears as I cried out to my brother, "I want to go home!"

25

Doniske comforted me as best he could, and when I finally stopped crying, he said, "We are going home, little Maria." I looked up at him, surprised. "Home is where your family is," he said, hugging me tightly. "And soon your family will be in America."

As I looked over the railing, I saw the most wonderful sight I had ever seen. LAND! At first it was only a green line, but then it grew bigger. As our ship pulled into New York harbor, people crowded on deck to stare in awe at the tall buildings.

28

As I walked down the gangplank toward America, I turned to Mama and said, "Mama, I discovered something during our journey." Before Mama could ask what it was, I continued, "Doniske helped me learn it. I've discovered that it doesn't matter where you or your ancestors were born. It doesn't matter where you grew up. Home is where your family is."

Katie (Kathleen Anne) Kavanagh, author of **Home Is Where Your Family Is**, lives with her family in Newton, Massachusetts, a suburb of Boston. Her father, Robert, is a computer specialist for the Belmont Public Schools. Her mother, Carole, works at home as the coordinator of the nonprofit Boston Association for Childbirth Education. Katie has an older sister, Meghan, and a younger brother, William.

Katie's favorite subjects are language arts, social studies, and science. She enjoys reading, writing, swimming, bike riding, counted cross-stitch, baton twirling, and dancing. In addition, Katie plays soccer and softball and enjoys watching major-league baseball. Katie likes the Florida Marlins, but her favorite team is the New York Yankees.

Katie wants to be a veterinarian and an author. She loves animals and has two fish named Diamond and Speckle. No matter how busy she is, Katie always finds time for reading. Katie especially enjoys fiction. Some of her favorite books are *Blitz Cat*, *The True Confessions of Charlotte Doyle*, and *Incident on Hawk's Hill*.

As a fifth-grade student at Horace Mann Elementary School, Katie was sponsored in the Publish-a-Book Contest by her language arts teacher, Mrs. Lorraine Field. The idea for the story came from a program on immigration that was presented at the school. Katie's great-grandparents immigrated to America from Russia, Italy, and Ireland. Like the characters in the story, they came in search of a better life.

The twenty honorable-mention winners in the **1993 Raintree/Steck-Vaughn Publish-a-Book Contest** were Aimee Lillie, Marenisco School, Marenisco, Michigan; Angela Livengood, Christie Elementary, Plano, Texas; Alison Dick, Milford Public Library, Milford, Indiana; Tres Blackshear, Wellington School, St. Petersburg, Florida; Kim Thatcher, Tipton Middle School, Tipton, Indiana; Amber Luttrell, Leeper Middle School, Claremore, Oklahoma; Anna Searle, Ballard Elementary, Niles, Michigan; Courtney Kirkpatrick, Shady Oaks Elementary, Hurst, Texas; Meg Cochran, Denton Public Library, Denton, Texas; Amanda Yeager, Midland Trail Elementary, Diamond, West Virginia; Callie Weed, Venice Christian School, Venice, Florida; Sam Rodriguez III, Farmington Elementary, Germantown, Tennessee; Audra Burns, Cutler School, South Hamilton, Massachusetts; Arwen Miller, Brimfield Elementary, Kent, Ohio; Beth Darwin, Iuka Middle School, Iuka, Mississippi; Jason Mathews, South Davis Elementary, Arlington, Texas; Amy Michael, Franklin Community Library, Minneapolis, Minnesota; Brett Harris, Germantown Academy, Ft. Washington, Pennsylvania; Bethany Valandra, Bethesda Lutheran School, Hot Springs, South Dakota; and Cailean O'Connor, Edgewood School, Scarsdale, New York.

Gregg Fitzhugh, a graduate of the Maryland Institute College of Art, has illustrated advertising and promotional pieces as well as books. He has received numerous awards, including the Associated Press Gold Medal.